I WISH I WERE BIG

For Nicola – remember, small is beautiful

I WISH I WERE
BIG

PETER BOWMAN

RED FOX

A Red Fox Book

Published by Random House Children's Books
20 Vauxhall Bridge Road, London SW1V 2SA

A division of Random House UK Ltd
London Melbourne Sydney Auckland
Johannesburg and agencies throughout the world

3 5 7 9 10 8 6 4 2

First published in Great Britain by Hutchinson Children's Books 1997

Red Fox edition 1999

Printed in China

RANDOM HOUSE UK Limited Reg. No. 954009

ISBN 0 09 969271 6

I'm hungry.
It must be lunch-time.

I'm too small to reach.

Oh, thank you.

I wish I were as big as a mouse.

Well... maybe not!

Wow!
I could never climb
that high.

I wish I were as big as a cat.

Well... maybe not!

I'm not big enough to jump that far.

Goodness me!

I wish I were as big as a dog.

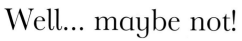

Well... maybe not!

I'm hungry again.
If only I could fly!

Hey, it's easy for you.

I wish
I were as
big as a
horse.

Well... maybe not!

I wish I were
as big as an
elephant.

Well... maybe not!

I'm glad I'm small.